W9-CEL-351

SKELLY
the Skeleton Girl

SIMON & SCHUSTER BOOKS FOR YOUNG READERS
An imprint of Simon & Schuster Children's Publishing Division
1230 Avenue of the Americas, New York, New York 10020
Copyright © 2007 by Jimmy Pickering
All rights reserved, including the right of reproduction in whole or in part in any form.
SIMON & SCHUSTER BOOKS FOR YOUNG READERS is a trademark of Simon & Schuster, Inc.
Book design by Lizzy Bromley
The text for this book is set in Stanyan.
The art for this book was created using mixed media.
Manufactured in China
10 9 8 7 6 5 4 3 2
Library of Congress Cataloging-in-Publication Data
Pickering, Jimmy.
Skelly the skeleton girl / Jimmy Pickering.—1st ed.
p. cm.
Summary: Skelly the skeleton girl finds a bone lying on the floor of her house and wonders where it came from, and when she finally finds the answer, she is pleasantly surprised.
ISBN-13: 978-1-4169-1192-0
ISBN-10: 1-4169-1192-8
[1. Skeleton—Fiction. 2. Bones—Fiction. 3. Dogs—Fiction.]
I. Title.
PZ7.P55252Sk 2007
[E]—dc22
2006004023

To Julian Chaney, the best pal this Skeleton Boy has ever had!

SKELLY
the Skeleton Girl

Written and illustrated by
JIMMY PICKERING

SIMON & SCHUSTER BOOKS FOR YOUNG READERS
New York London Toronto Sydney

My name is

SKELLY.

I'm a skeleton girl.

This is my HOUSE, high on a hill.

I found a BONE
lying on my floor.

I asked my FISH
if it was his.
"No, the BONE'S
not mine."

I asked my BAT
as we went for a stroll.

"No," he said.
"Does it belong to YOU?"

Could it be a BONE from me?
No, it wasn't mine.

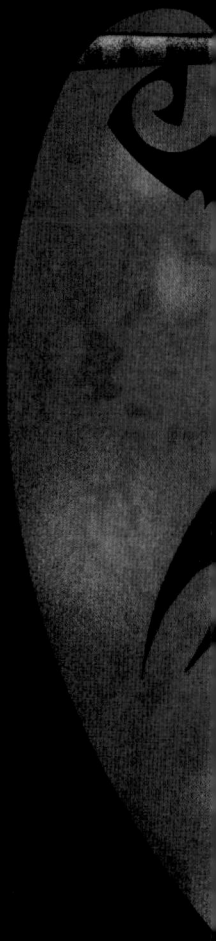

POWER FACTOR
X-RaY

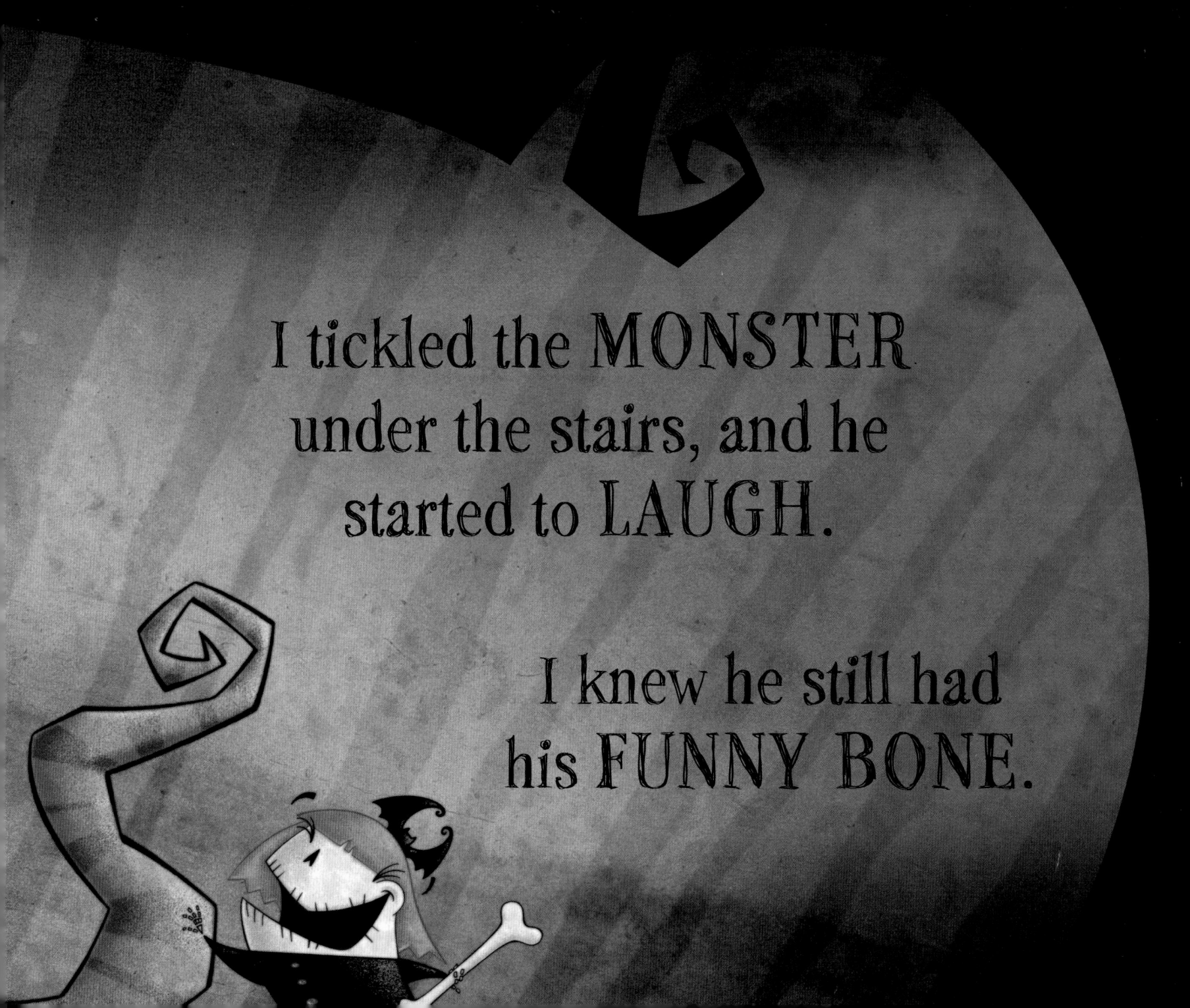

I tickled the MONSTER under the stairs, and he started to LAUGH.

I knew he still had his FUNNY BONE.

1
3

I asked my
MAN-EATING plants.

"No, my dear,
we wouldn't
eat THAT!"

I asked the GHOSTS who came to tea
if it belonged to them.

"Honey, we have no BONES."
"We lost those long ago."

I asked the SPIDER
who lived next door
if it could be his.

"No, my dear.
simply put,
we SPIDERS
don't have BONES."

X

I checked my dolls from
HEAD to TOE. . . .
They hadn't lost
a STITCH.

This bony search was
making me HUNGRY.
I went to the kitchen
for a piece of CAKE.

That's when I heard a
NOISE
outside my window.

I ran
past my FISH,
past
my BAT,
past my
MONSTER,

past my
MAN-EATING plants,
into the
GARDEN.

I peeked around the TOPIARY HEDGE to see what the NOISE could be.

"Does this belong to
YOU?"

I found the owner of the BONE,
and I found a new
FRIEND, too!